The Adventures of Jimmy Neutron BOY GENIUS

The Time Pincher

by Ruth Koeppel
based on the teleplay by Jed Spingarn
illustrated by Natasha Sasic

Ready-to-Read

Simon Spotlight/Nickelodeon
New York   London   Toronto   Sydney   Singapore

Based on the TV series *The Adventures of Jimmy Neutron, Boy Genius*™
as seen on Nickelodeon®

SIMON SPOTLIGHT
An imprint of Simon & Schuster Children's Publishing Division
1230 Avenue of the Americas
New York, New York 10020

Manufactured in the United States of America

First Edition

2 4 6 8 10 9 7 5 3 1

Library of Congress Cataloging-in-Publication Data
Koeppel, Ruth.
The time pincher / by Ruth Koeppel.—1st ed.
p. cm.—(Ready-to-read ; #1)
Based on the teleplay by Jed Spingarn.
Summary: To prove Cindy does not know what she is talking about, Jimmy uses his special "time
pinch" machine to bring Thomas Edison to the present.
ISBN 0-689-85293-2
[1. Inventions—Fiction. 2. Time travel—Fiction. 3. Science fiction.]
I. Spingarn, Jed. II. Title. III. Series. PZ7.K81823 Bi 2003
[E]—dc21   2002006223

In Miss Fowl's classroom
Cindy gave an oral report.
"So Mr. Marconi invented
the radio in 1870," said Cindy.
Jimmy raised his hand and
said, "But Thomas Edison
didn't harness electricity until
TWELVE YEARS LATER!"

"Maybe Marconi's radio didn't run on electricity!" Cindy said.

"Right. I forgot about the radio powered by mud!" Jimmy replied.

"Saying Thomas Edison's name all the time doesn't prove you right!" Cindy yelled.

Jimmy asked Miss Fowl if he could be excused, and he zipped home on his jetpack backpack.

"I will give her proof," he muttered.

"I know time travel is risky, boy,"
Jimmy told his dog, Goddard.
"But I will just prove my point
and send him right back.
Initiate time pinch!" commanded Jimmy.

A green glow filled the booth.
Suddenly a strange man appeared.
"It's Thomas Edison!" Jimmy gasped.
"That's right, shorty," said the man.
"Now, what's going on?"

Jimmy explained everything
as he drove Edison back to school
in his hover car.
"Whip-diddly-doo!" said Edison.
"This hover car is a piece of work!"
"Thanks!" said Jimmy.

Jimmy burst into his classroom.
"Jimmy!" exclaimed Miss Fowl.
"Ladies and gentlemen," Jimmy shouted.
"I give you the world's greatest inventor—
Thomas Edison!"

Edison faced Cindy.

"So you are Cindy, eh?
Well, the radio wasn't invented until 1893.
It couldn't have happened
without my electricity!" he said.

"Thanks, Mr. Edison!" said Jimmy
as the bell rang. "Now you probably
have a million questions for me—"
"Jimmy, maybe your friend would like
to see the town?" Miss Fowl said,
interrupting.

"I accept!" Edison said.
"But I have to send you back!"
Jimmy called after him
as they hurried out the door.

An hour later at the Candy Bar,
Jimmy, Carl, and Sheen found
Miss Fowl and Thomas Edison.
"Come with us to Retroland, Jimmy,"
said Carl.

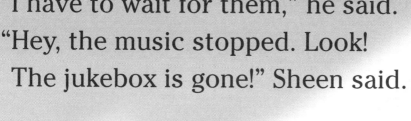

Jimmy shook his head.
"I have to wait for them," he said.
"Hey, the music stopped. Look!
The jukebox is gone!" Sheen said.

"This is terrible!" said Jimmy.
"I have let Edison stay here
too long! Everything electric
is disappearing!"

Then Jimmy noticed Miss Fowl
and Thomas Edison were gone.
Outside he saw them in-line skating!
"Mr. Edison," Jimmy called,
"I have got to send you back
or everything electric will disappear!"

"I am not going back," Edison said as
Miss Fowl grabbed his hand.
"He's about to get a face full of
Jimmy Neutron!" Jimmy yelled.

Back at the lab Jimmy strapped
a solar battery on Goddard
so he wouldn't disappear too.
Then he read the list
on Goddard's video screen.

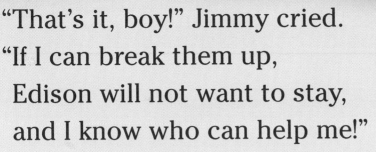

"That's it, boy!" Jimmy cried.
"If I can break them up,
Edison will not want to stay,
and I know who can help me!"

1 : Convince town that
electricity is overrated

2 : Change name ...
flee country

3 : Break up Edison
and Miss Fowl

Jimmy asked his parents about love.
"When I first met your father, he looked like Prince Charming in his shoe-salesman uniform," his mom said dreamily.

"And you were Cinderella
in search of a slipper
for your plump little footsies,"
his father told his mom.
"My feet aren't plump!"
his mom yelled.
"Hmm . . . ," Jimmy murmured.
That gave him an idea!

At Retroland, Carl and Sheen
rode the new Bat-out-of-Heck ride.
"This is wild!" Carl screamed.

Suddenly their car stopped.
They were stranded upside down!
"My blood is going to my head,"
cried Carl.
"Mine too," Sheen said. "Cool!"

Back at his lab Jimmy spoke
into a walkie-talkie. His voice
sounded just like Thomas Edison's.
Goddard barked.
"It's just me, boy!" Jimmy said.

"See? I put a voice transformer inside," he said, explaining.
"This is going to help me break up Edison and Miss Fowl!"
He tossed the other walkie-talkie to Goddard and told him the plan.

At the park, while Jimmy
hid in a tree, Thomas Edison
read Miss Fowl a poem.
"'Roses are red, violets are blue,'"
came Edison's voice. "'Miss Fowl's
armpits stink like a heap of skunks!'"
Miss Fowl leaped to her feet.
"How dare you!" she cried.
"Wait a minute!" said Edison.
"I-I didn't say that!"

Then Jimmy lost his balance
and dropped his walkie-talkie!
"*You* made me say those things!"
Edison said as he caught it.
"I had to break you up so you'd
want to go back!" Jimmy cried.
"My pits do not stink?"
Miss Fowl asked.

"They are . . . perfect! Want to
get married?" asked Edison.
"Oh, Tom. I am not the marrying kind,"
Miss Fowl said sadly.

"Well, Jimmy, I guess I have
to go home," Edison said.
"How did you build
that doohickey anyway?"
"It was nothing," Jimmy said shyly.
Thomas Edison grinned.
"Yeah?" he asked.
"Smart kid!"

TIME BOOTH TIME BOOTH